A Book of Shorts

Stories from Various Drawers

Joy A. Burke

A Book of Shorts
Stories from Various Drawers

CROOKED TAIL PRESS
www.crookedtailpress.com

© Copyright 2014 Joy A. Burke

All Rights Reserved

This book or any parts thereof may not be reproduced or transmitted in any form by any means—electronic or otherwise—without the expressed written permission of the author and publisher, except as provided by United States of America copyright law

ISBN-13: 978-1-946380-14-2

Published by Crooked Tail Press

Cover design by Joy A. Burke

For Shawn.
You make all my dreams come true.

Table of Contents

The Break In

I could have avoided all that trouble if only I had remembered to lock the back door. In fact, I didn't even shut it. My wife, June, is always on top of these things but she is on vacation until this evening visiting her parents in New Mexico and I was in a hurry to get to the dentist. Emergency root canal. But, when she sees the vase I gave her for our 20th anniversary in pieces – I'm banking on getting points for at least remembering to open the door to let Sesame – our cat – outside.

This is one of those times having a video camera running at strategic point throughout the house would have been great. Not only to have helped piece together what happened, but to pull it off the shelf on movie night and sit back for a good laugh. It would have been a hit.

Absolute chaos greeted me when I unclosed the front door and stepped into the entryway. At first, I thought I wasn't seeing clearly. After all, the root canal was a rough procedure. But no, it was true. Cushions off the sofa, chairs knocked over, drapes not where they ought to be. Not to mention the beloved antique vase I bought for my wife seven years ago lay in pieces in the hallway, flowers trailing toward the staircase. Dare I go upstairs? I could see past the hallway into the kitchen and dining area and see the vandalism was the same. Yes, vandalism was what this was and who knew if they were still inside. I could barely make out the sliding glass door that still stood ajar. I felt my vision may be starting to blur. My tooth was still throbbing. I was in no shape for this. I quietly stepped back outside and called 9-1-1.

For the six minutes I stood waiting for the police, my thoughts kept drifting between my tooth and my wife returning in only a few too-short hours. How was I going to clean this mess, file a police report, and try to glue together an Antique Chinese vase before my wife walked in the door-when all I really wanted to do was go back to bed and pretend I hadn't been the victim of a home invasion and I was born with perfect teeth like my wife.

Officer Meyer led the way back toward my entry from the curb where I was waiting. At least I think it was officer. Maybe it was detective, but I kept calling him officer and he kept responding. At any rate, I would've hoped the dental drugs would've been wearing off by now, but somehow I think they were just starting to kick in. It seemed to take us an enormous amount of time to establish nothing was stolen (probably because I really hadn't looked) and that I didn't have any enemies (despite the fact my house was just ransacked). I was impressed how this combination of experiences was making the 52-year-old man I last thought I was, want to cry. Office Meyer suggested I wait downstairs while he and his partner checked out the rest of the house. My tooth sent a surge of compliance through my jaw. He headed upstairs.

A short time later he descended with an amused look on his face.

"Do you own any pets, Mr. Leeder?"

A strange question considering the state of my house. But

then the light came on…they've ransomed Sesame! My tooth gave an affirming throb.

"We own a cat, yes. Why?"

"I think you'd better come see this." He smiled and led the way back up the stairs to the guest room. Thinking the worst, I followed.

There, on top of the maple armoire was Sesame, fast asleep but looking a little frazzled nonetheless. Below her, a sleeping sentinel was the neighbor's chocolate lab, Ox.

I Believe

I believe in the power of freshly baked bread.

When you walk into a home and aromatic swirls of fresh bread tickle your nose, you can't help but smile and be transported to another time.

A time, perhaps, where your mother or grandmother removed fresh rolls or bread from the oven and pulled the first flaky piece off just for you. Or a time where you walked into a bakery filled with pastries and bread varieties glistening in the warm glow of their cases; Sourdough, French and Rye tantalizing your taste buds from afar.

There's something about a fresh loaf of bread that sooths the soul and lets us know that not everything has to be done at high speed. The way the butter melts into the bread encourages us to savor the slice. Let our saliva do its job.

Some things still take their time.

Bea by the Window

"I can see two days' worth of meds hiding under your Kleenex, Mr. Chatterly." He watched the young nurse finish folding the fresh linens and lay them at the foot of the bed, where Peabody the cat sat observing. Before he could get a word out in his defense, she was at him again. "Now I didn't say anything yesterday because I hoped you'd come to your senses, but I can see you're going to give me trouble. I'll be back with your lunch in a little while, William, and I expect this morning's pills to be taken when I return." Closing the door half way as she exited, Nurse Know-It-All, as he liked to call her left him feeling grumpier than when she arrived.

"It's the damn cottonmouth, Bea. She'd understand if *she* took these blasted pills." His expression softened as he looked over at his wife sitting in her favorite wing chair by the window. But, as always since their automobile accident, she simply smiled and said nothing.

"All right, all right. You always did get your way with me." He paused long enough to give her a wink. "I'll take the pills. Then I'll get out of these casts and build you that birdhouse." He stretched out a bruised, sun-spotted arm toward the water bottle on the nightstand but couldn't quite reach. He looked toward his wife, beautiful in her gray hair.

"What anniversary was that for? 40th? 50th?" He pushed his still muscular arms to the limit as he moved himself a few inches closer to the bed table. That outta do it, he thought.

Just as he began to reach out, a tuft of fur brushed his

side and two great green eyes gleamed up at him.

"Peabody, you're blocking my reach." The orange cat's only response was to begin to purr and rub against Williams side. "Bea, would you call your cat, please." No response. "Honey, please. He's been all over me since we came home from the hospital. Aren't you feeding him?" When she still sat there, eyes twinkling, he sighed and smiled back, pushed the cat aside and tried for the water once again. In a single painstaking motion, his fingers touched the water bottle enough to tip it onto the floor and under the bed sending a wide-eyed Peabody leaping after it.

"Did you see that, Bea?" Frustrated, William leaned back against his pillows. As he saw it there was only one solution. Throwing off the heavy quilt, William scooted himself closer to the bed's edge. He stretched out one arm to brace himself against the wall and clutched the bed with his other, tattooed arm. William breathed deep, bracing himself for the pain as he slid himself to the floor. It was an awkward task, but he managed to pull his broken legs after him and lay exhausted on the hardwood.

Peabody trotted over purring and rubbed his side up and down Williams face. He finally settled with squinty eyes on William's chest.

"You are all manners of a pest, Peabody." Once again he gently moved the orange cat aside then made the effort to readjust his position. There, just about an arm's length away under the bed, was the water bottle.

"Peabody, please! Get out of the way!" The fluffy orange cat, purring contentedly found his way in front of Williams face and under his hand.

"Bea?"

His fingers blindly touched the bottle and it spun against

the hardwood floor out of reach. Peabody's eyes dilated as he pounced after it, sending it spinning away even further.

"Bea?" He called exasperated. "Bea, I can't do this on my own."

"Mr.Chatterly!" The nurse quickly put down the lunch tray and rushed down to where William lay on the floor. "What are you doing down here? Are you hurt?"

William looked up at her, forcing the tears to stay where they were.

"I was just trying to get the water bottle so I could take the pills and get these casts off. I told Bea I'd make her birdhouse as soon as I was better."

The nurse reached around the bed to where the bottle now rest and handed it to William.

"And what did Bea say?"

"Nothing. She just sits in her chair and smiles. Ever since the accident. She just sits there and says nothing." With shaking hands he undid the cap and took a drink. The nurse handed him the pills which he took obediently.

"Mr. Chatterly, William," She waited until he was looking at her. "Do you recall your wife's injuries?"

The tears he'd been holding back slowly started to trickle down.

"Yes."

"Sir, I'm sorry, but…"

"I can't do this on my own. We've never been apart."

The nurse screwed the lid on the bottle for him, then brought his lunch and sat on the floor next do him.

"You won't be, Mr. Chatterly. I'll be here with you."

When I Was A Child

When I was a child I saw a window in a field. It was clear and strong and showed me a vision of a land I didn't recognize. A strong breeze blew by and swept me through the window and I tumbled down far into that land. And as I gazed upon it I stood tall and was not afraid because I knew it was where I belonged.

Thanksgiving

For my first Thanksgiving as a host, I bought the biggest turkey they had in the store. Eyebrows raised around me as I hefted that baby into my cart and I even got a few nods of approval from nearby men. It was plain on their faces they wished they were headed to my house for Thanksgiving.

As I collected the trappings for my feast the mixed aromas of spices succulent and sweet tickled my nostrils in anticipation. This was going to be good. Given the amount of time it took to unload the car, I may have gone a little overboard in my attempt to impress. That being said, once the cooking got started it was a relief not to worry about needing or running out of anything.

Now, I'm no Julia Childs, but I know how to read and follow directions so I had this turkey thing in the bag make no mistake. I make a list, check it twice, shop with a mission, read the directions, set out the necessary supplies and ingredients like a platoon waiting for orders and get to work. And that's exactly what I did.

The first warning sign there might be trouble should have been the look on my husband's face when I hauled in the turkey; the second, his subsequent remarks.

"What is that?"

"Well, it's a turkey! And a beauty at that isn't it! You should have seen everyone's face when I rolled this thing in the cart."

"I bet. How do you plan to thaw, dress and cook 'turkey beauty'? You *have* seen the size of our oven, right?"

Hm. Of course I had; and hadn't given it a moment's

consideration when picking out my prized turkey. Daniel gave me a sympathetic look followed by an encouraging smile.

"Let's run some water and thaw it in the tub. It should be done in time to cook before people arrive tomorrow."

We took turns long into the night draining and refilling the tub (and mopping up the overflow) to thaw out the turkey.

Success arrived around 3am. Enough time to throw it in the fridge for the last bit of thawing and get a few hours' sleep before the real fun began.

My army of ingredients and utensils stood at attention as I tied on my apron Thanksgiving morning, ready for me to plunge into the stuffing and side dish creation. It wasn't long before the house smelled of stuffing, Green Bean Casserole, mashed potatoes with cheese, deviled eggs and pickled beets. We had managed to stuff the turkey, then stuff the oven with the turkey and now all we had to do was tidy, wait and baste.

Daniel had just arrived with Molly, our 2-year-old retriever, back from their morning run as I was getting ready for another round of basting. Being her energetic self, Molly bounds over my direction for slobbery kisses but is clearly distracted by the variety of smells from the countertop. I swear it was mid-leap she turned toward the counter to take a full-on whiff and her paw caught the side of the casserole dish. The momentum of the casserole dish was enough to whack the pickled beets like a queue ball and magenta goo and beets went flying with green beans close on their tail.

With an astounding crash, the hardwood became the resting place for the conglomeration of pickled beets, Green

Bean Casserole and the pieces of blue and gold glass dishes that held our sides. I ran for towels and wet rags, terrified the pickling dye was about to stay with us permanently; Daniel ran after Molly trying to beat her paws to the glass fragments; Molly, not realizing anything was amiss and delighted with the homecoming results bolted for the fresh dinner on the floor.

Once the floor had been mopped up and salvaged, Molly's paws given a clean bill of health and the tears had tried a bit, the hilarity of the situation came to surface. Remembering I was going to baste the turkey almost an hour ago, I headed back over to take care of our main dish. At least that couldn't fall off a counter.

Upon nearing the oven, the sick feeling of dread started to creep over me. Even when I baked cookies, I could feel heat radiating from it. Right now, there was nothing. Opening the oven confirmed my fears. No heat wave washing over me, no Turkey dinner smells, no wisps of burnt trappings on the bottom - nothing. The oven was dead.

"Oh no! What are we going to do?"

"Why? What happened? Did it spill over?" Daniel was by my side before I could finish my exasperated sigh.

"No, none of that. The oven is not working," to prove my point I stuck my hand near the heating element, then touched the luke-warm turkey. "I know it was earlier. I made the potatoes and green beans!"

"The turkey is rather large, Sophie, and more than consumed the oven," he sat down beside me on the kitchen floor and put his arm around my waist to draw me close. "Besides, our poor old oven probably got tuckered out with all that hard work you were forcing it to do in one day."

We both took another look at the obscenely large bird in our cold oven.

"Do you think it would fit on the BBQ?" Daniel shot me a kind but skeptical look.

"Not likely. There's not nearly enough time to cook it out there, not to mention there's no propane. Go fish."

I puzzled together in my brain my last shopping trip, what I brought home, what we already had and what we could do with it. People would start to arrive in just a few hours and I had to have a plan. In fact, a plan was already taking shape.

We spent the rest of the morning and early afternoon cleaning the kitchen and rest of the house and making the transition to being thankful for what we have and for each other. And of course putting the turkey back in the fridge. I snuck some decorations and clove and pumpkin scented candles out for the occasion as well, if nothing more than to remind myself it really was Thanksgiving.

The time finally came and the guests poured in. It was so great to see everyone, the tension from earlier that had started to subside, vanished completely. We all sat around the table and shared what we were all thankful for. At the top of my list was a husband who loved me, quirks and all, and a home to live in - even if the oven stopped working on Thanksgiving Day.

And that's why we all ate hamburgers and turkey stuffing, for our Thanksgiving dinner.

The Benefactor

When I first told my family about the enormous wedge of cheese left outside our door, they didn't believe me. We had just moved into the neighborhood and no one seemed friendly, let alone inclined to offer food to strangers — especially in these hard times.

After much coaxing I finally convinced them to take a look for themselves and help me determine whether or not it was a trap left for us or if it was safe to bring into the hole-in-the-wall we now called home. It sat there innocently enough, tempting each one of us with its succulent aroma — but we had to be objective. There were no large objects nearby for would-be thieves to hide behind so we felt safe from robbers; no signs we would be kidnapped and sold or just plain tied up and tossed out somewhere and our new home taken over. Another good sign. After further inspection, we deemed the cheese a miracle and towed it in dreaming all the ways we could make use of cheese in a meal.

Over the next few weeks we received regular food bundles from our unknown benefactor. We longed to know who it was that continued to make our existence in the miserable little community bearable but no matter how we kept watch, they did not make themselves known, and we did not see them. It was as if they food came down straight from heaven.

If it wasn't enough we were the poorest family in the area, no one would interact with us more than absolutely necessary because we all had white hair. I suppose they felt like that made us prime targets for kidnappings and such, at least that's what my father always said. But I think we just made them uncomfortable. We were just different and they didn't know how to react. When I was little, I only had one other friend who looked like me; all the other kids had dark hair. She and I got along so well and had the best of times because we understood how it felt to be on the outside of things. But then she didn't come to school one day and my mom only said she had gone away and I wouldn't be able to see her again. Everyone else said she had been taken or kidnapped and stayed clear of me like it was contagious, and I was going to be next. Shortly after that, we moved. It's been that way ever since.

I think it was a Tuesday when I looked out a hole through the front wall and saw another bundle waiting to be brought inside. Delighted, I hurried outside and did a brief and in all honesty, careless check for any trickery before picking up the highly anticipated food. What would it be today? Bread or cheese? Or just like last week we were given the smallest variety of meats! I looked out across the road and felt a slight air of smugness as I watched my fellows scurrying about on their hard day's work. They may look down on us, but here I stood out of the heat because someone out of the goodness of their heart had compassion on us and did not discriminate when all these others did. As I opened the bundle, to my joy I saw not just bread or cheese, but both! With a sliver of meat on the side! But as I rejoiced, I did not see the shadow that crept down on me as I stood out there in front of my hole-in-the-wall where, had I taken my father's advice, I would have taken the food gifts inside to open. But too late did I look up and see a monstrous human face smiling, putting a bag over my entire body.

"Enjoy the goodies, my sweet," he said tying off the bag. "It's off to the pet shop for you."

And that's how I ended up in Bernie's Albino Rat Shop.

Standing Here Naked

You know when you are in a dream and you feel its reality, but you still somehow know it's a dream. Well, this wasn't one of those times. And I would have given anything if it were.

Lies can get you in a bunch of trouble; even if you are trying to do the best thing for your family. I didn't even mean for it go this far, but I was trying to save face and allow my child to belong – allow *myself* to belong. And we did; until Shirley had to go snooping.

Well, you know how it goes…one minute you're standing here enjoying life and what it has to offer. The next, you're standing here naked, everything laid bare for all to see. Shamed and hurt by the downcast eyes and backs that face you.

I don't know where we will go to now. But we will go. We always do.

Navel vs. Rind

Have you ever seen that Malibu rum commercial where all the islanders line up to buy melons at the fruit stand? You can't see me but I'm there. I must be there because no matter where I go or how hard I try some cosmic force prevents me from getting the melon of my dreams. Where with the islanders in the commercial there are melons every which direction — but for display purposes only, I just can't manage to get my hands on a good melon. Man, I just want to buy a melon!

Healthy eating is a foreign realm for me, I hate to admit it but that's the way it is. However, my husband and I are making strides to incorporate healthier foods into our chicken, bread and chocolate diet. We thought we'd start small with fruit. It still has sugar.

I have great memories of eating cantaloupe with my dad in my younger years. He had and still has this uncanny ability to pick the most mouthwatering melons. I swear they see him coming and roll to the front of the heap just so he'll take one of them home and sprinkle salt all over their glistening insides. Conversely, in a normal year, my husband and I may get about ten servings of fruit. Gasp! I know. Most of that is when we spend vacation with our nieces who love watermelon and honeydew. I'm not sure what the chemical reaction is in my brain, but it is so much more satisfying when I don't have to cut it up. Or clean it up.

With that in mind, we really are trying to add more fruit to our dry pallets. So, since melons have been tried and true for the past ten servings this year, I decided to buck up and start my shopping in the produce department. You can imagine my delight when a fellow shopper at the local grocery offered to assist me in selecting produce. In fact, it wasn't so much an offer, it was more he made a B line in my direction as soon as he walked through the door, was chuckling as he arrived at my side and asked,

"Excuse me, but what on earth are you doing?"

I of course, thought it was obvious. But laughing and trying to humor him I replied, "I'm trying to pick out a cantaloupe! I thought if you pushed and smelled the navel you'd know if it was ripe."

The gentleman then proceeded to get quite scientific about choosing the perfect cantaloupe by feeling the weight versus the size and pressing on the rind to see how hard or soft it was. Apparently, the goal is to choose a melon whose weight is equal to its size so it will be juicy and ripe. But not too heavy- or it will be over ripe. That's why he was pressing the rind; too soft, no good. As any good teacher would, he gave me plenty of melons to test out and decide for myself where they ranked. No navel smelling involved. I kindly thanked him for his assistance and, after selecting a cantaloupe, I scurried off to the bakery where I felt more at ease.

Once home and confident in my selection, I wasted no time slicing my prize into bite size pieces. The melon unfortunately was not as delicious as I had hoped and was left soggy and uneaten in the fridge. I was therefore forced to resume with the bread and chocolate regime.

Later that week, I visited my dad and shared this story with him over a perfect cantaloupe on the back porch. My dad, who always picks the perfect melons, (and always smells the navel) had never heard of the scientific melon picking method. Not to say it doesn't work and isn't personal preference it simply did not work out for me. But if faced with a cantaloupe again, and it's navel versus rind, I'm going to go back to the navel.

However, that still leaves me back where I started.

I have no idea how to pick a melon.

Three Strangers

The snow gently fell at First and Pine as a tall, dark haired young man pulled back his gloved wrist and squinted impatiently at his Quartz watch. 1:56. The bus was three minutes late.

"Don't worry. It'll come." The young man turned to see a lean, young man like himself stretched vertically on the bus stop bench grinning mischievously up at him, his brown hair hidden under a black beret, his pale hands resting on his stomach, and his wool trench coat touching the cool pavement.

"Hi. I'm Jason."

"Hello. My name is Andy." The words came out on a cloud of visible breath, as Andy reached out to take the extended hand, his watch shimmering in the afternoon light.

"Yup. There's nothing like a little bit of snow to perfect your day. But that bus will be here, don't you worry. It will just take a few extra minutes."

"Yes, well, my day is not running as seemingly perfect as yours, and I don't have a few extra minutes to freeze waiting for my bus." The nonchalant manner of his outgoing companion irritated Andy.

"Hey, you don't need to stamp at him like that. He's only making an optimistic comment." Surprised, the two you men looked to their left at the woman in her late twenties, leaning against the bus sign and crossing her arms.

Her bright brown eyes looked disapprovingly at them and her red lips were pressed in a frown.

"Well, I just need to get to the office. I have a meeting." Jason tried to conceal a smirk at the broken pattern in which Andy had attempted to excuse himself. He quickly turned his attention to the newest member in the conversation.

"Yeah, well snapping at people isn't going to get you there any faster." After looking at the two young men a long moment, she sighed and rolled her eyes. "Look at us, We're arguing like we're siblings.:

"What if we are." The young woman and Andy turned bewildered at Jason. The woman smiled.

"Yeah, what if we are?" She turned to see Andy's reaction.

"You guys are nuts." Turning away from their stares, Andy looked again at his watch.

"I'm Jason," Jason stepped toward the young woman, looking at Andy out of the corner of his eye and smiling, "Thanks for taking my side. What's your name?"

"Rose."

"Pleased to meet you, Rose. So, what if we are related—"

"Come on, Jason. Are you just bored?" Andy turned to face him.

"What's the harm? There's nothing better to do. Drift in the clouds a while, will ya'. It'll all go away." Recognition shot through Andy's face. "Whoa, Andy, you okay there?"

"That phrase, I've heard it before, just like that. It's so familiar."

"That's funny," Rose stepped toward the two, "so have I, and it really isn't that common of a phrase." An awkward silence fell upon the group.

"The last time I heard that was when I was in the Midwest almost twenty-three years ago," Andy took a seat on the snow-covered bench. "A tornado had just wiped out my entire neighborhood. A few of the people around survived, mainly children who had been stowed into storm cellars, but my parents didn't make it." Rose and Jason looked at one another and positioned themselves on the snowy bench next to Andy. "My brother, sister, and I came out from the cellar to devastation. We didn't recognize anything." Andy looked from Rose to Jason then to the soft snowflakes falling from the heavens.

"That night, we were taken to Child Protective Services. They told us that unless they could find someone that could support three children, we were going to be separated. We slept in a temporary foster home for the next few nights until permanent care for each of us was located. I still remember the room we all slept in. It had towering skylights and during the night, the moon illuminated the clouds that rushed in and out of our vision."

"And that when I said it, wasn't it," attention was given to Jason, "the three of us looked out at those clouds and talked about what was going to happen. And that's when I said it."

"Yes," Rose turned to Jason, "it was." A tear rolled down her face as she looked at the two strangers she had known all her life.

Cut!

It hadn't been a bad night. Pretty good actually; tips had been decent, people had been nice. I just only wish I didn't always smell like pizza. It always made me hungry. Thankfully, I was on my last stop then I could head home and get out of these clothes - after I nabbed my free pizza for the shift of course. I smiled in spite of myself. After two years delivering pizzas, the smell had finally gotten to me, but not the taste. Loved the taste…

"Here we are, Milo. 548 Hawthorne Street. Awful dark isn't it." I frowned at the stuffed dog smiling at me from the dash. No response. Figures. I pulled up to the house which thankfully had the porch light on illuminating the first gentle flakes of snow. Other than that, the street was completely dark. This was just on the outside of our service area and I had never been down here before.

"I certainly hope they get the streetlights fixed if they call back. Okay, keep the car warm. I got to take my keys so I can use the flashlight. I'm gonna lock you in." At this point I was talking more for my own sake, than Milo's. I grabbed the pizza carrier and headed out.

It was a nice night. Crisp and fresh smelling. By the time I rang the doorbell I was feeling a little cheerier. A dark haired, unsmiling man answered the door. I smiled.

"Hello! Pizza?" I started to pull the pizza out from its protective carrier as the door widened.

"Yes. What was the total again?" He flashes me a quick smile, more as an afterthought, and turns on the hall light as he heads to the nearby table where a wallet sits.

"Oh uh, $15.72 is the total." I wait patiently as he rummages through the wallet.

"Darn. I've got $10 here, give me just a minute to get a few more bucks from the kitchen. Is that snow? Please, step inside a minute. There's no need for you to wait outside in the cold. It would be poor manners of me to leave you out there – I'll just be a second." He smiles again.

I take a cautious half step inside while he turns and walks down the hall. It was cold. And the snow was starting to come down like it meant to stay. Inside, everything is dark as far the porch light illuminates. I can see beyond the entryway and a bit down the hall. I suddenly realize regardless of how long I've been standing here, this is against my better judgment. This is too creepy. I turn to look back out through the screen door and just as I reach to pull it the rest of the way open, something hard collides with the back of my head and the pizza and I go falling to the floor.

When I wake up, I'm tied to a chair by the hands and feet. There is no furniture other than the chair I'm tied to and the room is entirely dark aside from the single light directly above me. I smell pizza so I'm clearly still in my work clothes, thank goodness. But there's no gag in my mouth. So whoever has done this, is clearly not concerned about me calling for help. The floor is concrete and the room itself is cold. Must be a cellar or garage. It's then I notice I have a second shirt – a black shirt – over my work uniform. What is going on?

As if my thought demanded an answer, the door

which stood hidden in shadows, creaked open and the same man who answered the door for the pizza strode into the light.

"So. You thought you could get by us undetected using outdated CIA gear?"

I started blankly. What was he talking about? And why was he now talking with some sort of unrecognizable accent?

"Who are you really working for, or is the CIA really recruiting out of high school, fitting you with second-hand equipment, and considering you all expendable?" At this he gave a scornful laugh. "Well? Answer me!"

I could feel my jaw moving up and down but nothing was coming out. I was a mix of terror, confusion, and utter astonishment. Was this guy crazy, or was my luck seriously this bad to be confused with someone else?

"I'm a pizza delivery driver. I have no idea what you're talking about!"

"Cut. Cut!" A man in jeans and a t-shirt came through the door holding a bullhorn that said 'Director' on the side. "Anton, you said this kid was going to be the one! Are you telling me she doesn't even know her lines?!" He turns to me. "I don't know how long you've been acting babe. You've got the terror and confused look down, but if you want to be in this film you have *got* to learn your lines! Let's try it again. For heaven's sake Anton. I don't know where you get these kids from!"

Ramble

A talk with my friend about nothing in particular prompts me to look up "ramble." Having always used the word to refer to an almost pointless conversation, I am surprised to learn that it carries more than one meaning. People in conversation ramble, verb, vines ramble, verb, to take a ramble, noun. "Ramble", in fact, can mean to talk or write aimlessly, to spread in all directions, like a vine, and to take a walk or stroll.

In what we do on foot, rambling implies an aimless wandering, with the pleasant connotation that the very aimlessness of the ramble is something freely, even happily chosen.

The ramblings of a conversation seem equally as aimless, but are, it turns out, very regular in their irregularity— although if you were actually listening to someone talk about a serious thing, you might find that hard to believe. You would head in one direction, and then ramble elsewhere until you are going the opposite way, and then change topics again, following a conversation which turns upon itself and makes no sense. Could a psychiatrist or counselor, though, map you out the conversation you would see that what seems like chaos in the discussion actually forms a regular repeating pattern of reviewing the same issues.

The shortest distance between two points may be a straight line, but a frustrated person neither knows nor cares. They seldom carry on straight for a time of more than about ten minutes. An event erodes their banks of stability and control, and they way of the world is such that one side invariably erodes faster than the other. It eventually collapses and the emotions are carried along and deposited at a friend's feet. Two curves are thus begun: the erosion point becomes the outside of one; the emotions pile, the inside of the next.

The events on the outside have to occur evenly to keep up, causing more erosion, allowing more emotions to be expressed. The outside events get deeper, but the inside becomes clean and shallower. At any point, the shape of the person's character shows its history. If other forces do not prevent, the bends over time work toward becoming perfectly elliptical. "Ellipse" comes from the Greek for "to fall short", an ellipsis falling as it does short of a perfect circle.

This has all been observed in society and shown experimentally in friendships, and is thought by many to be sufficient explanation of rambles.

Others disagree, especially now that such a global community show that there are others—whose social banks have not been eroded—also ramble. Leaders and educators appear to ramble as well. Psychiatrists have calculated that the most probable path between two points in one's mind is in fact a ramble. Rambles then may be the norm, not the exception.

The question may be not why some people ramble, but why every person we talk to, does not.

This is a nod to 'Meander' by Mary Paumier Jones. An old college assignment—to emulate the beautiful flow and metaphor of the essay.

The Garbage Collector

Another frustrating day at work last week was topped off with the garbage, once again not being picked up. Apparently, it didn't matter how many times I called, wrote, or stuck notes onto the garbage toter, the guy did not want to pick up my trash.

Isn't that what it's all about? The customer? I mean, I *work* in customer service and the number one rule is the customer is *always* right. It's not like I'm making it up. It's been over a month and I have garbage piled up to the top of my fence! Every week I cart it out in extra cans and boxes for my garbage to be picked up *at my house!* Unless they want to pay me to go to the dump they need to come here and pick it up.

So, today I've taken the day off to sit here and wait for the driver to do whatever it is he does because he certainly doesn't pick up garbage, and then I'm going to confront him. And boy is he going to get it! My car is nicely tucked away in the garage, so he'll assume I'm at work. All is as it should be.

I can hear him coming. This is it! Oh, I can hardly wait to hear the excuses! There he is. But he's picking up the other side of the street. It seems I'll have to wait a little while longer. All that noise. You think they'd be able to make those trucks a bit quieter these days, but I suppose they do pack a lot of garbage. He's quite fast, isn't he? Already halfway down the street turning the corner and still manages to keep things tidy. I wouldn't have expected...what's this? Why is Morton Dawes sneaking from his side door and running across the street to—my garbage?! What on earth...he's pulling it back to my house! That little...

"Morton Dawes! What on earth are you doing with my garbage?"

"O! Um, hello, Sue. Home early?" Morton stepped behind the toter, placing the box of garbage he had been holding back on the ground between us, looking quickly down the street toward the oncoming garbage truck.

"Did you see me come home early? I'm here to figure out why my garbage isn't being picked up and I just figured out why! Who would've thought our own HOA president would want a pile of garbage outside someone's house? What is your problem?"

I already knew Morton was short tempered so how he became HOA president is beyond me, but he was starting to turn redder than a chili pepper.

"You are! You are always complaining, butting into other people's business and no matter how many times I send you letters you will not trim your grass and keep it up to code like the rest of us. I'm through with you! You've had a meeting and we are tired of having scum like you in the neighborhood, who we've noted can't even dispose of their household waste," he smiled smugly. "You're out!"

"You can't do that to me—I live here!" I had to scream over the roar of the garbage truck that had sat idling behind Morton while he gave his speech. Neither of us had noticed the large, muscular garbage man who had become our audience.

"So really, both of you are responsible for the harassing notes and calls I've been receiving—and over grass?"

With one sweeping motion, the garbage man threw Morton and Sue into the truck's box, lifted it high into the cloudless afternoon sky, dumped it, and they were no more.

Wishes

The postcard arrived with a heap of junk mail and I almost missed it. In the end it was the only worthwhile piece of mail in the lot. The front boasted an enormous brick building in the 19th century style—very beautiful. It was set cozily among trees showing their fall colors. Overall it gave off a very New England sort of feel.

Turning the postcard over to discover the location, I saw in tiny print it was the Camden-Place Boarding School for Social Etiquette (CPBSSE). But no location. I chuckled to myself wondering if there were *really* that many socially inept people out there to merit a mysterious school with no location. I personally, could only think of one—but surely being an adult, he wouldn't admit himself! Then again, he hadn't been at work in months...I quickly scanned the card for the sender. It *was* Michael Briggs! Well—it appears someone sent him. I started from the top.

Dear Jill,

You may be surprised upon receiving this postcard to learn of my acceptance into the CPBSSE. But I assure you, no one was more shocked than myself! I went to bed on the 22nd of February as usual and quite literally awoke here the next morning. It was like magic. I can't account for it happening at all.

The first few months were rather difficult. I got beat up a little and was constantly criticized every time I said anything. Can you imagine? Not to mention my penmanship being very poor and even the way *I spoke was 'abrasive' they said. I think the first day I was told I used harsh words and was told to mind my own business at least eight times. Outrageous!*

But I see I am lapsing into my old self again.

I just wanted to send a note to say I really had not quit work—I was in fact taken away! I do hope to be back and from what my instructors here say—by the end of next year, you should hope to find me much improved!

Best Regards,

Michael Briggs

I couldn't believe my eyes! My greatest wish had come true. The thorn in my side removed. Magic...could it have been? That very night he mentioned I'd lain in bed and wished for nothing more than for him to be corrected in every social faux pas he had as he was particularly rude and humiliating to a number of people including myself that day. Lo and behold—that was the last we saw of him. Now an explanation! Ha! I guess it just goes to show—you really *ought* to be careful what you wish for!

The Gift

I remain convinced my assignment to the dead letter office came as the direct result of what I thought was a clever remark to the postmasters attempt at a joke. Be that as it may, the dead letter office holds some surprising treasures. One such treasure I stumbled upon forever changed my life and the life of Gabriella Montgomery.

After my wife left me, I moved to New York for a change of pace and a new start. I never imagined the first woman I'd meet would be 72, still sweet on the eyes and become my closest friend. While a sense of melancholy surrounded Ella, the red-headed spitfire from days of old would appear as we'd people watch in the park and walk her Great Dane, Louie. So when I discovered the faded envelope addressed to her late one afternoon, I knew I'd come across a key to her hidden past and hoped she trusted me enough to unload some of her sorrows.

The envelope had a deep rich ivory color to it and felt pressed even after the multiple misdirection's it took and then decades of neglect. I took a moment to admire the incredible script on the front. Calligraphy? Or just thought and care taken while writing Ella's name and unique address. Something we've lost, I mused. Laser printers and sloppy penmanship. I imagined it smelled like something other than dust at one point; I wonder what?

"What've you got there, DeMask?" Implementing stealth mode, I slipped the letter under a lost boxed-up basketball and scooped them both under one arm as I turned to face Nosy Nelson.

"Nothing exciting here, Nelson. Just on my way to take this piece of lost and unclaimed mail to brighten a child's day. Did you have something for me — or perhaps there's something I can do for you?"

"Oh no, just thought I'd come over-" He trailed off as his eyes began to roam my desk.

"Off I go then! Have a great day and I will see you tomorrow." I waved as I backed out the door and caught a glimpse of Nelson starting his daily rummaging through my workstation. Who hires guys like that?

The short drive from the office to my apartment had me thinking about my new acquisition. How do I approach her? *Hey, neighbor I snuck a letter out of a federal building for you — it had your name on it after all — and thought you might want to share it with me?* Way too awkward. I set my keys and the letter on the kitchen table. I could be subtle. *Ella, I think I found something that belongs to you; a letter that was misdirected years ago.* She could sit down and read it here and I'll get her some tea.

What is wrong with me — what sort of friend am I? Besides, who's to say she'd even read it here?

I changed out of my work clothes, splashed water on my face and gave myself a good hard look in the mirror. I saw Ella. Laughing at Louie running after pigeons in the park, or at a joke I made or story about Nosy Nelson, but the smile never reached her hazel eyes. Always a hint of loss or regret. I sighed. I'm the type of friend who wants to see Ella smile with no reservations and see her trust me and share her life.

My ruminations were interrupted by the doorbell. A quick glance at the clock on my way out of the bedroom declared it to be 5:30pm. I wasn't expecting a dinner date, so I was surprised to find a woman bundled up outside my door with a steaming casserole dish and cupcakes dressed in pink and red.

"Ella? Hello!"

"Happy Valentine's Day, Allen!"

"What? Oh! Is it?"

"It is. Now, may I come in, or are you going to let an old lady freeze in this New York winter?" I stepped aside as she gave me a wink and walked in. I closed the door and caught the scent of roses and citrus. I could never tell which it was — the smell seemed to morph just when I thought I decided so I'd settled on it being both. I smiled and walked into the kitchen.

Ella was fingering the letter. Her coat draped over the chair, cupcakes on the counter and casserole still covered, she stood with her fingers just touching the envelope. My keys right next to it where I'd left them both earlier.

"Allen, where did you get this?"

Tea — I should get some tea.

"At work. I brought it home," she looked at me. "Well, yeah," I took a cautious step forward. "It seemed like it'd waited a long time to get to you — I was trying to help it find its way." She sat down. "Tea?"

"Yes, Allen, please. And why don't you start dishing up that casserole as well. I think you're right. Let's open this letter."

Yes! Tea, letter *and* dinner.

The casserole, of course, was fantastic. Everything she made was. I was already salivating over the cupcakes. But as I cleared the dishes, I was more occupied with Ella. She'd hardly spoken a word over dinner. Simply read the letter, lifted her chin, closed her eyes, set it down and exhaled. What does that mean? Bad news? Relief? Silent scary angry? I didn't ask, just let her be and refilled her Earl Grey. Based on my recent divorce, reading women's signals was not my forte.

"Did I ever tell you I was engaged, Allen?" I shook my head. "He was something else. Smart, kind, funny; boy could he make me laugh," she smiled as if recalling a joke — and this time her smile was complete. It spread to her eyes and they glowed, her cheeks were warm and flushed. She was beautiful. "But more than that, he loved me. *Me!* Despite my parents' protests and interventions, he was not dissuaded. We were going to marry." She looked to the letter then back to me her smile fading. "But he died, here in New York, in a car accident with my best friend. They found luggage packed and tickets for the boat headed to Quebec. What's more, they found a wedding ring. That's what set rumors flying. That they were eloping, and I had been duped." She chuckled once and leaned forward with her tea. "I could never believe it. My parent's lorded that over me until they died." She stopped talking for a time. I let her muse. Eventually, I couldn't handle it anymore.

"Ella, what's in the letter? You seem more at peace than I've ever seen you." She looked at me over the teacup.

"The truth. And yes, I am. Read for yourself." Gingerly, I picked up the folded page, and began to read.

My fair Ella,

*Come to New York! I have a surprise for you!
Maze and I have devised a plan that will surely suit
everyone – except your parents whom I'm afraid
will never sit comfortably on the idea of us being
wed. We will be at the docks at 10:20 this Tuesday
morning, November 16th with a justice of the peace
who will perform our vows. Maze has threatened
to kill if she's not a witness and I've another fellow
I know in town who will be there as well. We've
got bags packed and tickets bought. We're off to
see the world, love. All I need is you. I can't wait –
see you Tuesday.*

> *Much Love,*
> *Daniel*

I put the letter down and looked up to see Ella watching me.

"So, you were right all these years. You never gave up and this letter is proof he loved you to the end."

"Yes." She smiled that smile again, this time accompanied by a single tear. "How about those cupcakes?"

Gypsy

"It seems almost impossible for me to go back to that split second when I ran straight into that gypsy. It's been like dominoes ever since."

"I know, I know. But I'd really like you to try, Samantha. This has been a hurtle for you and I think if we can just relive the event, you can move on."

My therapist, Teareen is so patient. I guess that is why I am paying her $150 an hour. And that's the college-student discounted rate. Wow.

"Okay. So, I'm in New York waiting for the bus so I can catch my flight back here."

"And why were you in New York?"

"I was visiting a friend from school. I'd always wanted to see New York in the winter, and she invited me up."

"Okay, great. What happened next?"

"Well, I always get the munchies before I travel, and I spotted a vending machine before I bought my ticket. So I headed over to it. Out of *nowhere* this gypsy dressed in the craziest purple, lime green, and pink get-up, with nappy braids, jumps out in front of me and shoves an index card in my hand."

"And how did that make you feel?" What a typical therapist question. But she looks so sincere; brow furrowed, dark eyes looking all intent, olive skin radiant. I wonder if she
exfoliates...

"Well, I always thought I would scream in those situations, but I actually just kind of took a deep breath and froze. That's why I noticed she smelled so lovely. She smelled like snowflakes and freshly cut pine boughs. Really, despite her looks, she smelled a lot like Christmas to me. And her face was beautiful with the most incredible brown eyes I'd ever seen. You don't normally think of brown as being very remarkable, but hers were just entrancing. Seriously," I snapped out of my reverie. "I think she put a spell on me."

"Why would you think that?"

"Didn't you just hear the way I went on about here? That's totally creepy? I mean, it is to me."

Teareen smiled encouragingly. "I don't think it's creepy at all. What happened next?"

"So, she hands me this index card and says, 'Beware the skull and crossbones. The scissors will be your sign.' Then she squeezes my hand and disappears. I mean literally, I look at the card, see this mass of symbols, look up, and she's gone!"

I see Teareen jot down a few notes and review an earlier page. Am I the strangest case she's got? Or maybe the most amusing one? Maybe she doesn't believe me. Teareen must be a mom because she answers my question before I ask it and she can tell I'm looking at her.

"Don't worry, Samantha. You don't have to look so panicked," She finished her note and looked back at me. "I believe you. There are strange things that happen in the world. Most people just don't talk about them." She gave me one of her classic reassuring smiles. I think that's really why I pay the $150. To be reassured.

"Thanks, Teareen."

"You're welcome. Now, in an earlier session, you mentioned there were eight symbols on the card: a flag with nothing on it, a Celtic cross, a Yin-yang circle, a snowflake, a hand palm out sort of saying 'stop', a cursive looking 'n' trailing down with its tail making a partial infinity sign, the scissors, and the skull and crossbones. Is that correct?"

"Yep."

"And you mentioned a few minutes ago that it's been 'like dominos' ever since your encounter with her. What's happened? Have you seen any of these symbols play out?"

"Well that's the thing, isn't it? I'm *always* looking for them. I tried to just throw the card away, but then my superstitions got the best of me and I held onto it. I didn't even know I was superstitious. But for the past twelve weeks, I'm on the lookout for all this stuff. Everywhere I go, all the time."

"You still haven't answered the question."

Darn.

"Right. So, I was freaked out on the flight home and didn't tell anyone about it. But after a few weeks and nothing happened I figured it was just a bazaar situation. I went out to a bar with my friends one evening, to celebrate the end of finals you know, and I went to pay for my drink with the twenty I usually keep in my back pocket." Teareen gave me a disapproving look. "I know, not the best place to keep money. Anyway, what was there? Not the money, but the notecard. I'd completely forgotten about it and don't even recall putting it in my back pocket. But I opened it anyway and got a reminder of everything I'd happily forgotten. No sooner had I put it back in my pocket than some guy leans up next to me with a Celtic cross tattooed on his neck—just like the one on the card." I was honestly expecting more of a reaction since it unnerved me, but Teareen didn't seemed too phased. But there was more.

"So, after the guy with the tattoo gives me the stink eye for staring at him, I turn back to my drink which — well, guess," She looked up at me, but I didn't really give her time to respond. My nerves were splitting. "a flag! Yep, a flag with nothing on it. Normally, Grubb's has their little logo on their flags but not that night. I asked the bartender and she said they'd run out and had to get some generic ones. Go figure. That night, of all nights. Coincidence?"

"It's very possible, Samantha. And would you like some water? You're looking a little flushed."

Taereen handed me a water bottle which made the Excedrin go down much more smoothly. My head was pounding. I know I'm not going crazy, but reliving this stuff really stresses me out.

"Alright, so you saw two of the eight symbols. Have you seen any more?"

"Yes! I think it was about two or three weeks later, I went to a birthday party for Alisha, and another friend of hers I never met came over to say hi wearing the oddest pair of earrings that flashed. When I asked about them, she pulled back her hair so I could get a better look and one was a green snowflake the other was a pink and blue Yin-Yang symbol. I'm sorry Taereen, the ones at the bar may have been coincidence, but what are the chances of these two pairing up together to form earrings?"

Taereen looked a little puzzled as she wrote a few comments and turned her attention back to me.

"What happened next?"

"Nothing. I mean, I tried not to freak out on her or pull her earrings out and stomp on them. I was just polite, excused myself and spent some time in the bathroom trying to figure out what it meant. Am I supposed to be looking for the symbols to tell me something, or are they warning me, or am I supposed to respond in some way? I just don't know. What would you do?"

Taereen looked slightly surprised I asked, although I don't know why. She had to have seen that coming. Clearly, I'm lost, scared, and confused. It's not like I'm going to ask my mom—she knows all about that.

"Well, I'm not sure. And you know I'm not supposed to sway how you interpret your situation."

"Oh c'mon. Obviously, I don't know what to do! You've got to offer another perspective. Isn't that what you're here for—to give advice to lost youth?" Taereen laughed a little.

"Not quite, but I see your point. I guess I would go back to the very beginning. Consider how the gypsy made me feel, how I reacted, and what my gut sense of the situation was. Then I would go back to each time I came into contact with one of the symbols on the card and reflect on all those same things again. How they made me feel, how I reacted, and what my gut told me. Write them down. See what you come up with. That's all I can suggest, Samantha. It's what I would do."

I took Taerren's advice and started to write down all my feelings, gut reactions, and impressions ever since the gypsy handed me the notecard. Surprisingly, I discovered I felt the gypsy was warning me about something and every time I saw a sign, it was bringing me closer to whatever it was she was warning me about. Maybe she was my guardian angel with a horrible sense of style. That revelation made me feel a ton better. My $150 an hour was paying off.

The rain poured so hard on my way to work, I was starting to worry my car wouldn't hold up under the pressure. Break lights lit up in front of me and I slowed, stopped, and squinted to see what the hubbub was about. Construction crew. Kind of strange. Well, maybe not. They have to work in all weather. I neared the man with the stop sign, which he somehow dropped which the car in front of me took as a go-ahead to drive on. So instead of picking up the sign he waved his arms at me and pushed his palm out, fingers splayed clearing telling me to stop. The fifth sign.

Well, they always come in twos. Where's the other one? I turned my windshield wipers on maximum to see what I could see. It didn't take long. Past the construction workers, on a brick building was a variety of graffiti. Some of it absolutely beautiful. One sort of strange design made from purple, pink, and lime-green stuck out at me. The artist's tag was a cursive 'n', its tail turning into a partial infinity sign.

"Move it! I'm already late." A honk and a shout carried over the thundering rain and into my car. *Impressive pipes.*

I waved in my review mirror and moved forward. That left the scissors and the skull and crossbones. What was she trying to warn me about?

"Hey Sam, thanks so much for walking with me. I really want to lose some weight before the wedding and lunch seems to be the only time I can fit it in."

I looked Alisha up and down. Seriously? She loses any more weight she's going to blow away if someone sneezes.

"No problem, Alisha. Happy to get out of the office for a bit. Where are we headed?" It really was nice to stretch our legs for a while, get out and laugh. Working as a paralegal was great, but kind of stuffy.

"Oh look! A ribbon cutting. I wonder what's opening. Let's go take a look. I always think those giant scissors are totally ridiculous."

I froze.

"What did you say?"

"A ribbon cutting. Let's go see what's opening." I looked to my left to where Alisha's glittery-blue fingernail was half-heartedly pointing. An enormous pair of pink scissors lay against a panel of glass windows just a few shops away. "Are you okay, Sam? You're turning really pale. Let's go grab a seat by the fountain."

"No! We have to get out of here. C'mon." I grabbed Alisha's wrist and caught the crosswalk across the road and pulled her into a small café smelling of croissants and jam at the opposite end of the street as the ribbon cutting.

"What is going on, Sam?"

"I don't know. But I think I will soon. They always come in pairs." I looked past Alisha's concerned face down the block where the pink scissors still leaned against the windows.

An old, dented black Cadillac sped past the café, through the red light and crashed into the fountain Alisha and I had been standing by moments ago.

"Oh my gosh," Alisha pressed her head against the window along with everyone else in the café. I leaned back in my chair and breathed out slowly, closing my eyes.

"Thank you," I whispered.

Opening my eyes, I saw woman in a purple, lime-green, and pink dress with braided hair and the most beautiful brown eyes smile at me from across the street. Then, she was gone.

Condiments

I was bested by the girl with the ketchup bottle.

Hardly fair. All I had was the Tabasco sauce and it barely has any words on the label. I clearly overestimated my ingenuity.

Our town holds a picnic every year with all sorts of kiddie rides, games, great food, and crazy contests. Like this one—the 'Condiment Squeeze.' The goal of course, is to take as many words from the label of your assigned condiment and put them into a creative piece, crossing them out as you go within the time limit.

I'd been preparing myself for this contest for months. Lining up all the condiments I could think of across my writing desk and getting to work. Never did I think of Tabasco sauce as a condiment. Who uses that? But looking back, what else would it be?

Had I been clever, I would have been taking an inventory of the condiments over the past few years, but I didn't think of it because for the last four years I'd won! It had been with mayo, mustard, relish and horseradish. And before be, Kelly won with ranch, pickles, and may as well. Even before Kelly, Sherwin won with ketchup and Soy Sauce—but that was before my time. The point is, no one ever won the 'Condiment Squeeze' with Tabasco sauce.

But there's always next year. And you can bet your best bees' knees that I'll be prepared, even if I end up with syrup.

Acknowledgements

I would like to thank my husband, Shawn, for believing in
me and giving me the courage to move forward.
This would have never become a reality without him.

Thanks mom and dad, for being the eyes that see where I
am blind, and your compassion to help me become a better
person.

John, thank you for helping cultivate my creativity.
There is no better brother or friend.

Butch—I haven't forgotten about you.
Thank you for always asking about the book. You were my
constant reminder that someone, somewhere, was waiting
for it.

And to my dear friends and writing accomplices:
Thank you for your encouraging spirits!

To My Readers

Thank you for taking the time
to read my collection of shorts!

If you enjoyed this book, I'd love to hear about it.

Let me know what you enjoyed and
what you thought could use some tweaking.
Email me at ideas@joyaburke.com.

If would like to know when my next compilation of short
stories is coming out, visit www.joyaburke.com to sign up
for alerts, clips, sneak peeks, and other fun stuff!

Thanks for spending some time with me. I look forward to
creating more stories you can enjoy and relax with.

You can also keep touch online via Twitter:

@joyaburke

www.ingramcontent.com/pod-product-compliance
Lightning Source LLC
Chambersburg PA
CBHW032043180726
48284CB00008B/2732